ALICE IN WANDERLUST

FORMERLY PUBLISHED AS DOUBLE TROUBLE IN LOVE AND FIREWORKS - A NEW YEAR'S EVE NOVELLA

ANNA FOXKIRK

FLOCK PRESS

FOREWORD

Alice in Wanderlust was first published as a novella entitled, *Double Trouble* in the New Year's Eve anthology *Love and Fireworks*.

Published by Flock Press

Copyright © 2021 by Anna Foxkirk

The moral right of the author has been asserted.

All rights reserved.

No part of this publication may be reproduced in any form or by any electronic or mechanical means, including information storage and retrieval systems, without written permission from the author, except for the use of brief quotations in a book review.

All characters and events in this publication, other than those clearly in the public domain, are fictitious and any resemblance to real persons, living or dead, is purely coincidental.

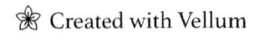

❀ Created with Vellum

1

"Alice? You still here?" Roger hollers from somewhere in the bowels of the pub.

I pause, a bead of perspiration trickling down the side of my face. Hands immersed in hot soapy suds, I'm in the kitchen out the back of the Jolly Roger Inn scrubbing at pie crust that's superglued itself around the edge of a dish. I listen, puffing at my hair flopping into my eyes, uncomfortably aware of perspiration itching along my hairline and trickling down the sides of my face.

Roger is silent for now, so I resume my scrubbing.

Twister, my twisted twin sister (more fondly known as Tilly by our parents) is proving about as easy to shift as this oven-baked grime. If only I could figure out how to persuade her it's time we moved on. Our year traveling together has ground to a halt. Catching glimpses of my reflection in the window above the sink isn't helping the head of steam I'm building up about our predicament. I want out of Sydney; Tilly seems to have become welded to the place.

I glance again at the clock on the wall. Everyone else has already left the building, except for Roger, the owner of this shithole, and me. I've only been working here for three weeks, but it's been long enough to figure out Roger is only *jolly* when the occasion suits him or when laughing at his own inappropriate jokes. It's amazing that any sane woman would find him remotely attractive, but only last week, Kylie, one of my co-workers confessed, with a snigger, that she'd let Roger have his jolly way with her in a cubicle of the Ladies'. The very idea makes me nauseous. To my mind, Roger's not so much a Jack Sparrow, as Kylie would have us imagine, as Jack Rodent, a scurrying scurvy bilge rat sniffing out his next victim.

If only I'd had the gumption to refuse to work the additional shift this week but lured by holiday rates and the need to pay rent on our apartment (because Tilly never seems to have a cent to her name), I've now worked five consecutive days since Christmas. Roger's take on my situation is that as the new kid on the block I'm not in a position to negotiate, but —Ho, bloody ho!— 'positions are always negotiable'.

I do not want to dwell on the greasy smirk on his face when he said those words, nor the fact he's becoming increasingly matey.

After drying the pans on the draining board, I throw everything back in the appropriate cupboards as fast as I can. Unfortunately, a pan lid clatters to the floor with all the discretion of clashing cymbals.

I freeze.

Whistling and footsteps head in my direction and the hairs on the back of my neck stand to attention as Roger swaggers in.

"Ahoy, my lovely! Still here? Anyone would think you were reluctant to leave me."

"Just finishing off," I say, hurriedly wiping down the worktops, my skin prickling as he leans against the doorframe and studies my every move. How is it, I wonder for the gazillionth time, that Tilly can land a glamorous job singing with a band and serving cocktails in a flashy nightclub, while I'm stuck sweating over dishes and fending off the scourge of Sydney? Oh yes, it probably has something to do with the fact that Tilly is screwing the nightclub owner, Axel.

"Fancy a nightcap, doll?" Roger winks.

I'm never exactly sure if he's calling me *doll* or *darl*, but either way I'd rather walk the plank. "Thanks, but I'm knackered. Not tonight." Not any night.

Drying my hands on my apron, I hang it up. As I shrug into my denim jacket and sling the shoulder strap of my handbag over my head, I'm aware of Roger pulling on his beard. I know I'm nothing to write home about, especially not in my current swampy state, but the way he's eyeing me up you'd think I was drop dead gorgeous.

A thick hairy arm bars my exit from the premises.

"Right. See you tomorrow then," I say.

Roger doesn't budge.

Panic fluttering in my chest, I consider my options. Sadly, I have none of Twister's acerbic wit or tongue-lashing confidence. Despite being her identical twin, she's the sort of siren who can sink a man with a heart-piercing glare or lure him into her arms (and bed) with a provocative whisper. We may be twins, but as far as my understanding of men goes, she was born fifteen minutes and about a hundred light-years ahead of me.

"Come on, Bucko! The night is but young," says Roger.

"I'm exhausted. Roger, excuse me. Please could you let me pass."

Slowly, miraculously, he moves enough to leave a tiny fissure through which I can squeeze, but as I rush towards it, his arm shoots out again. I skid to a halt, my heart skittering.

"I've been meaning to ask, when are you and me going on a proper date, Alice?"

I titter nervously. "Oh, I don't know. We're both busy people." *Maybe when Darling Harbour freezes over.*

"And busy people need to have fun. Look, I've done the roster for the next few days. I put you down to work during the day on New Year's Eve, but I've given you the evening off." He grins exposing yellowed teeth. "We could splice the mainsail together."

Excuse me? I gag. Or at least mentally, I gag. I have no interest in splicing anything with Roger. But how to talk my way out of here? "Well, thank you. That sounds like an interesting idea, but I—"

"Great. I'll hold you to that. I'm working on pulling in a few favors, pulling a few strings ..." He taps his bulbous red nose as if he has a great secret. "If all works out, maybe that won't be all I'm pulling. We'll bung some fire in the hole yet, eh?"

I don't know about fire, but I'd like to put a rocket under him and blast him into the stratosphere. The man is a monster. I glower at him. "We can discuss this some other time. I'm too tired to think straight right now...I'm. Going. Home," I say annunciating my last words very deliberately.

There is a rumble beneath our feet — perhaps an articulated truck passing by or a small earthquake — enough to rattle the plates and dishes on the shelves and for Roger to be momentarily distracted.

Taking full advantage, I dash beneath his arm quicker than a rat can flick its tail. As I rush through the gap, a hand connects with my backside and a low jeer of laughter follows me out of the restaurant onto the dark street.

Creep!

I break into a run and don't stop until I've rounded the corner of Dalgety Road. I gasp for breath. *I can't believe the disgusting rat slapped my backside!* I'm furious and ashamed. I should report him to someone ... but who? And what would that achieve? I'd be out of a job, and even if I've no intention of staying any longer than I have to there are still bills to pay. What I need to do is persuade Twister it's time we were moving on. Sooner rather than later. Find work elsewhere. I can't stay at the Jolly Roger – scrubbing dishes is the least of my worries.

Glancing over my shoulder, as I continue to jog up the street, I can't help worrying that he could be following me. Imagine if Roger knew where we lived. Where *I* lived. A shudder runs through me. Ugh. God forbid.

Tilly has more or less moved in with her clubbing boyfriend. I don't really blame her. It must be much nicer sharing silk sheets and a king-sized waterbed with Axel, than sharing the lumpy futon and cramped studio flat with me. Still, I can't help wishing she was around a bit more.

If wishes were horses, beggars would ride. Mum's voice in my head makes me smile and I finally slow down to a walk.

The last time I saw Twister was Christmas morning. I made the mistake of bringing up the subject of our truncated gap year and travel plans, and a row exploded between us in spectacular festive fashion. It's nothing unusual for the two of us to bicker, but that had been about as close as we've come yet to going our separate ways – something I promised Mum would never happen. For all the stress and headaches my sister gives me, I adore her. It's about time I called a truce. Or at least attempt to make contact with her.

I take out my cellphone and call her, but she doesn't answer. Maybe she's still pissed off with me. Maybe she's too busy having a life. Maybe it shouldn't always be me having to—

All holy crap! I leap out of my skin as something darts across my path and hisses — a bloody cat.

My heart pummels against my ribcage and I bend double trying to catch my breath. "Bloody scaredy cat!" I yell after it.

A sob escapes me.

It takes a few deep breaths and a stern talking to myself and blowing my nose, before I get my nerves back under control. If anyone was watching me they'd think I'd lost the plot entirely.

I start walking again and my legs feel like jelly. I wanted this adventure, I remind myself. I wanted nothing more than to see the world and live ... but some days I feel like I might as well be on my own. I never realized traveling with Twister would mean spending so much time alone.

2

Reeling from the ammonia stench in the elevator, I hold my breath until it reaches the eighth floor where we live. The doors open and, having held my breath the entire journey upwards, I burst into the open corridor, gasping for fresh air.

A distant siren and traffic from the street below filter through the humid night, as I trudge past the closed doors of neighboring apartments until I reach ours. The smell of cigarettes greets me. I smile because it means Twister is here.

I can't stand her smoking, but the sight of my sister leaning over the railing of our minuscule balcony, puffing away, is a joy to behold.

"Twister!" I kick off my shoes, hang up my jacket and drop my bag on the sofa.

But when Twister looks over her shoulder, my mouth drops open. "Shit, Tilly! What's happened?"

Her eyes are red and puffy, mascara smeared. She stubs her cigarette out on a saucer cupped in her hand. Maybe now is not the best time to have a go at her about that as well.

"Where've you been? I've been waiting ages!" she whimpers.

"I've been at work. Crap, what is it?" I throw my arms around her, holding her tight as sobs begin to shake her thin frame.

"Oh, A-A-Alice! He ... he ... he ..." She can't even get the words out.

"Hey, don't even think about him. Everything's going to be fine, okay? Whatever's happened, we'll make it right." I hold her fast, stroking her back, murmuring sisterly assurances into her nicotine-smelling hair. And I can't help the small vine of hope which begins to unfurl and wrap itself around me. Maybe this means we're finally done here. Maybe we can move on. "I told you Axel was a no-good piece of crap. What's he done now?"

"He-he threw me out!" she wails.

Hooray. "What a wanker! Axel threw *you* out? He must be mad."

She sniffs. "Madder than a cut snake, apparently. I wasn't even allowed to see him. To explain. He wouldn't even let me into the club to talk to him!"

"What a tosser!"

That starts her off again. I can't remember when I last saw Twister this bad. But to be honest, on the inside I'm already skipping around the flat, packing our bags, booking tickets out of here. With a concerted effort, I compose my face and look sincere. "Don't worry about it, Tilly. You can stay here tonight, and once we've paid the rent we owe, we can hit the road again. It'll be amazing. A whole new adventure! This is a great news. It means we can ..." I trail off because her wailing has become louder than a whole colony of cats.

I let her cry. Sometimes with her, it's better to let her get it out of her system. After much shushing and more hair-stroking Twister's sobbing finally subsides. I get up and fetch paracetamol, a glass of water and tissues.

"Thanks, Malice. You smell hideous by the way," Tilly mutters.

Yeah, so like I call Tilly, Twister, her nickname for me is Malice. And sometimes evil Alice McMalice.

"I smell hideous? Says the woman who reeks of cigarettes and booze. You don't exactly look too hot yourself."

Our bickering makes me happy for the first time in days. This banter is so much more like us – a good dose of verbal abuse is a sure sign of our sisterly devotion. While Twister swallows the pills, I sniff the front of my t-shirt. It's true, it's rank. I stink of cooking fat, fish and chips, and sweat. And possibly Roger – the very idea makes me want to crawl out of my own skin.

"I need a shower."

"You need a life. I don't know how you can bear working in that crappy bar," says Tilly.

"Because it's a job and we need to pay the rent, and while we're on the subject—"

Twister blows her nose noisily, and I figure now is maybe not the time to exert pressure on her with regards our shared financial obligations. In theory she should stump up half the rent; in reality, I'm prepared to pay the lot and forego the deposit if it means we can get the hell away from here, but I need to stick it out at the Jolly Roger at least until I'm paid what I'm due for this week ... The thought of going back there makes me break out in a cold sweat.

I make Twister a mug of tea and we curl up together on the sofa.

"Sorry, I've not been around much lately. Do you hate me for deserting you?" She pokes me with her toe.

"I loathe you," I say, smiling at her over the brim of my mug.

"Love you too." She stares wistfully into her tea. "I miss Mum and Dad."

"Me too ... though having come all this way, I'm still desperate to see Australia. We've hardly been anywhere yet."

"And I'm ruining your big travel adventure." She chews her lip.

This is true, but I sip my tea and keep *schtum* for all of thirty seconds.

"Not for long, Twists. Now we can hit the road," I say, smothering a yawn and noticing my hands resemble raw sausages ... and my back is killing me. Before I go anywhere, I need sleep and lots of it.

"I'll hand in our notice on the flat," I say, "and once we get this month's rent paid, we can— "

A knock at the door interrupts me.

Tilly spills her tea, as she plonks it on the floor. She looks terrified, nudging me with her foot and gesturing at the door. "It could be one of Axel's men. Or Axel. I can't see anyone looking like this! You go!" she hisses.

Honestly, she's so vain. And I'm too tired to argue. "Okay. Keep your hair on."

Putting the chain on the lock, I open the door a crack.

There is a guy standing outside and he definitely isn't Axel.

3

"Hello," I mumble through the crack. *Oh hello!* He's hot. He's beautiful. Enough to make me want to shrivel up because I look like a dirty dishrag.

"You going to let me in, Tilly, or what?" he demands.

I'm used to people getting the pair of us confused. We are as identical as identical twins get, so it's an easy mistake to make, unless you know us: Twister has all the style, panache and gumption; I have all the self-doubts, social awkwardness and emotional constipation. It's not really a fair split.

"Hold on." I close the door again. "What d'you want me to say?" I look around. "Tilly?" I hiss.

Tilly has shot across to the other side of the room and is now hiding around the corner of our bed alcove. Although I only caught a slivered glimpse of the guy, despite all my reservations, I would have happily let him in, but Tilly is shaking her head, and gesticulating slicing her own throat, stabbing her finger in the air at something invisible.

I tiptoe over to her.

"Tell him I'm not here and to go away. Or tell him it's too late. Tell him I'm sick. Tell him *anything*, just get rid of him," she pleads.

I scratch my head. "You do realize it's not Axel. This guy looks ... nice." Nice is an understatement. Knackered though I may be, one glimpse of all that disheveled manliness has woken me right up. He's a vast improvement on Axel. This guy, I could understand hanging around in Sydney for.

"I don't care. Get. Rid. Of. Him."

"Okay. Fine!"

I stalk back to the front door and clear my throat before opening it a crack. *Oh Lord.* Sending this bloke away is enough to make me want to weep. "Um ... so sorry, but I'm just going to bed ..." There's a spark in his eyes that makes me want to buckle. Him and bed seem like the ideal combination right now — after I've showered, obviously — but I've Tilly to consider.

I sigh. "I'm tired and it's kind of late."

"I just wanted to know you're okay." He leans closer, eyeballing me through the narrow gap. It's a disconcerting eye. Smokey grey with amber flecks and eyelashes to kill for. "Axel doesn't worry me," he says, which I think is kind of awesome. "Besides, I've given you both my word, haven't I?"

His word on what exactly? "Hmmm, I know. Axel's a complete dickhead, but—"

"But it's no reason for you to miss a rehearsal. We've only got one more practice session before our big night, and you swore you'd stick it out this time. You said you were cool as."

Cool as what? Why do Aussies never finish their similes? And what the hell is going on here?

My brain does a loop the loop trying to make sense of everything. "I am cool. Cool as a cucumber." Which is not a cool thing to say. I'm the sort of cool as a cucumber that's been left in the fridge for month. "But I think I may have caught a chill." In summer? In Australia? "I feel a bit woozy, you know, and light-headed." Ain't that the truth — he's enough to make any woman's head spin.

His eye narrows with suspicion. Or is it scrutiny?

"Sorry, I'm truly sorry ... All I need is some bed rest and I'll be back on my feet and back to normal. Tomorrow is another day, but for now ... regrettably ... I need you to leave me in peace."

"Perhaps I should come in and take your temperature," he murmurs. "I want you alive and kicking for New Year's Eve. I want ... Don't look at me like that. I swear I'll behave."

Behave? I'd rather he misbehaved. I bite my lip and remind myself I smell like a kitchen waste disposal unit. But oh, the horrible, wicked temptation. If Twister were not here and I were not a complete loser. There's more than a little irony in my wishing her away when not an hour before I'd been wishing her here. Is this bloke an employee of Axel's? Is that why she doesn't want to see him? He has the pecs for it and he does look vaguely familiar.

I hold up a finger. "One minute." Closing the door on him again, I shuffle back to Twister.

"Are you absolutely sure? Who is he?" I whisper. "He wants to come in. It's not too late to change your mind. I could sleep on the sofa ..."

My sister has her fists clenched, her eyes squeezed shut and her face screwed up. "No! It's Guy. He heads up the band."

"What RiffRaff?" That's the daft name of the band Twister has started singing with, although there is nothing RiffRaff about Tilly. Even grimacing and red-eyed she manages to look a cut above the rest of us mere mortals.

"Yes, Guy Balcombe, duh! I'm not seeing him looking like this," she repeats, glaring at me as if I'm stupid. Which I'm not by the way. My school results were way better than Twister's, but then, not surprising as I always had so much more time for studying. Anyway, it explains why the dude looks familiar. I've seen publicity shots of the band, but they don't do him justice; he is even more beautiful in the flesh.

"What's happening on New Year's Eve?" I ask.

"Some charity function on a mega motor yacht. For community heroes. Don't you ever listen to me? I told you all about it already!"

I'm pretty sure she hasn't.

"Just tell him, I'll see him when I'm feeling better!" Tilly insists.

More fool her. Rolling my eyes, I return to the door.

"Well?"

"Sorry, Guy, I'd love to let you in, but there's a chance, I think I'd better isolate until I've tested." I give a little cough. "I may be contagious." I bloody wish. There is nothing contagious about me; Tilly is the one who brings men out in a fever. "I have a thumping headache and a sore throat ... If I'm going to sing, I need to look after myself. You don't ... really help the situation."

He leans against the door and blinks at me. Thankfully, the safety chain holds his weight. And I block his view into the apartment as best I can (without getting too close).

"Can I get you anything?" *Can he...?* The pitch of his voice has lowered to an intimate purr. It has a molten quality to it that makes my stomach swoop. If he were crooning into a microphone, I can imagine there'd be a lot of jelly-kneed women lying at his feet.

"No. I've everything I need. I'm sure I'll be okay by tomorrow," I croak. Once Twi-Tilly has come to her senses, the daft bat.

"Right. You do look kind of bushed."

Cheers for the reality check.

I don't have to act weak-kneed, what with that hypnotic stare and tranquilizing voice. I'm stupefied, fed up Tilly wants me to get rid of him, ready to drop because I'm bone-tired and now I can't help thinking wistfully of bed ... wishing I had one jot of Twister's charisma or confidence, so I could drag him into it with me.

One thing's for certain. Nothing's going to keep me from going to watch RiffRaff before we leave Sydney. I'll be there come hell or high water, ogling from the front row. Maybe Twister could get me a ticket for this New Year's Eve bash, whatever it is. Maybe I could be the band gopher.

"Do you honestly think you'll be able to make it to rehearsal tomorrow? If not, we need to find a replacement pronto."

I glance over my shoulder, but she's disappeared from view. I put a hand to my forehead. "I'm sure I'll be fine. Remind me where again ..."

"Tilly, for fuck's sake! I've been texting you about it all day."

Though he sounds more than a bit snippy, he manages to smile, and my heart crumples a little more.

"My phone battery died."

"Oh. That explains it. Sorry, I'm a bit stressed about New Year's Eve, that's all. It's gonna be big. You never know who could be there."

"Of course!" I forgive him instantly, as any sane woman would, and watch as he scribbles something on a scrap of paper.

"Here. That's the change of address, now we can't rehearse at the club seeing as Axel has, you know … Anyway, I'm not here to make you feel even worse. I was really hoping we …" He pauses and huffs out a breath. "Ah, shit. Never mind. Just text me if you're still not feeling well enough tomorrow. I'll sort everything … though you know I think you're irreplaceable."

Two high spots of color brighten his cheeks. As he pushes the piece of paper through the crack, our fingers brush and electricity zaps up my arm. I snatch the paper and try to close the door, but he holds it open.

"I'm sorry for what happened, Tilly. I never meant to dump you in the shit like that. I hope you forgive me." His expression has become tender enough to melt metal. "It won't happen again. The band needs you."

Just one more guy in lust with my sister. How is it I can look so like her and yet have entirely failed to inherit an atom of her sex appeal? "Okay. Bye." I close the door and lean my weight against it. *Crap!*

After a second his footsteps fade into the distance.

That was intense. He was intense. And I'm so jealous of Twister, I'd quite like to throttle her.

"I'm going for a shower," I say marching past. "I'm cream-crackered."

"Hmmm," she replies. She's too busy texting to even thank me, but that's Twister through and through.

In the shower I decide next year is going to look a whole lot different to this year: I'm going to grab life by the balls, I'm going to live every day as if it were my last, I'm going to out-twist Twister…

Alice in Wanderlust

But when I return to the bedroom, my best laid plans immediately nosedive. Twister has her suitcase on the futon and is throwing clothes in.

"What's going on?" I ask.

"I can't stay."

I can't honestly blame her. As far as real estate goes, this is not much better than a hamster cage. I collapse on the other side of the mattress. "Where? Please, not back to Axel. Please, no."

Tilly doesn't answer. She's struggling with the zip of her suitcase, and I'm not about to help her.

"I thought Axel had thrown you out?" I snap.

She grunts, but doesn't answer.

"Why are you crawling back to him? Are you a glutton for punishment, or what? Twister, he's not good for you, you know. Have some self-respect!" Like I can talk. But still … "You shouldn't be going back to him like a bloody boomerang. Spend the night here, and I'll speak to him in the morning for you. With or without you. Whatever you prefer. I'd come with you right now, but I'm too deadbeat."

I'm rewarded with a fleeting smile as she lugs her suitcase off the bed. "I don't want you going anywhere near Axel."

Beg pardon? "As if I'd be interested in him." As if he'd be interested in me! But I can see Tilly's as sensitive as blue touch paper tonight and the last thing I want to do is to light her fuse.

If she had any sense, she should run after Guy.

I pass the scrap of paper at her. "That's the change of address for your rehearsal tomorrow. Don't forget." Flopping back on the pillow, I close my eyes, conjuring up Guy's troubled face. That electric touch. If only I'd been showered and—

"I can't," Twister says.

"You what?"

"The rehearsal. I'm not doing it."

"Why the hell not? You can't let his band down like that." Suddenly I'm the noble champion of RiffRaff? "I wish you'd tell me what the hell is going on."

Twister's eyes brim with tears again. "It's a long story and like you said, you're tired. Me too. I need some time out and space to think without you influencing my decisions." Me influencing *her* decisions? "I need to get my head straight."

And then some. Why would she pick Axel over Guy? "Going back to Axel is like putting your head in a hungry tiger's cage."

"Yes, I know. I'm not going back to him, I swear, but...but...Life's complicated and right now it happens to suck big time." Tilly grabs my hand and hauls me upright.

I grimace feeling about as lively as a rag doll. "It's you who always complicates things," I grumble. "If you hadn't fallen for Axel in the first place, we'd be on the road right now. If you would only—"

"Malice, I don't need a lecture, alright. I know everything you're saying is true, but all I need right now is a hug." She pulls me into her arms. "I'm really honestly sorry. Alright?"

All my resentment melts away. I can never stay angry with Twister for long, besides I'm not fit to argue with anyone when I'm this worn out.

"I want you to do me a favor," she pleads.

I groan.

"Please, Alice." This is more like the Twister I know and love. "Like what?"

"Be me for a while."

Oh no. Not this again. "Twister, no! You can't be serious. Please, no."

Tilly gives me her pathetic puppy face. "Please, yes." She cups my cheeks between her hands. "Play me like only you know how. I need you to buy me some time. Sing for me. You know you have a much better voice than mine."

We've been known to swap identities now and again, much to our parents' dismay. It rarely works out well. Twister even let me pretend to be her with a boyfriend when we were teenagers once, but I'd been so freaked out when he tried to put his hand up my skirt on a bus that we'd been thrown off. I blew the whole relationship, and Twister and I didn't speak for a whole week. And then there was the Cosmo incident...

"I can't play you. Not with Axel. He's terrifying." No way with Axel. The thought of that tattooed hulk coming anywhere near me is even more scary than Roger the Pirate.

"You don't need to go anywhere near Axel. Just be with the band. Be with Guy. Just for a couple of days. Please, Alice. Pleeeease!"

The fact that she's calling me Alice not Malice says something. And I may be a little harsh at time on the outside, but Twister knows how to soften me up. The thought of spending time with Guy makes me marshmallow. Spend time with him and the band? Hmmm. What a tricky decision.

"I'll love you forever," she says.

"Okay. Fine." I say, trying to summon up some inner grumpiness. Inside of me, a little will-o-the-wisp fairy light has just ignited and started prancing around the studio.

"You're a trooper," says Tilly dragging her suitcase towards the door. "I owe you one. The playlist is on our Spotify. Try to not sing better than me. And don't get too operatic. And try to enjoy yourself, Malice. Live a little."

4

The next morning the sun streams in through the window as if it's the most glorious day. I can hear a kookaburra laughing and though I'm only half awake, it makes me smile. For a happy few seconds I envisage going to Bondi Beach, swimming and surfing, checking out all the super hot guys. I stretch like a smug cat. And then I remember I'm meant to be working at the Jolly Roger that day. *Ugh.* And the events of the previous evening return with a jolt. *Double ugh.* What the heck do I do about Roger?

I sit bolt upright. *Oh crap, and Twister!*

Sometimes, I don't know whether to love or hate my sister.

With a groan I text her.

> Hey Twister, how're you feeling this morning? When are you coming back? When are you coming to your senses?!! You don't really want me to do this band rehearsal thing for you today, do you?

There is zero response which I take as a sullen yes.

On the plus side, it means I get the satisfaction of texting Roger to say I'm unwell and cannot go into work today. And if I get paid ... It feels like a step in the right direction. A positive step towards a better me and my New Year's resolution to say 'no' a bit more often. After Roger's performance last night, it's a relief not to have to go anywhere near him — Roger can jolly well cope without me.

My fingers itch to hand in my notice altogether, but not yet. We can't afford to dip into our savings and the rent on our shoebox is extortionate. Plus, I've put in way too many hours to not get paid. I'm not jeopardizing all that blood, sweat and tears for nothing.

I text Twister again asking her to at least remind me of the songs I need to learn for the 'big night' … but all I get is more radio silence. How am I meant to pretend to be my sister if I don't even know what I'm meant to be singing? I trawl my memory for songs I've heard her practicing in the flat with her audience of one — me. She'd even dragged me to listen to her in the stairwell of the apartment block once — the acoustics are better — until some neighbor yelled at us.

Then I remember her mentioning her Spotify list.

Thank God for small mercies. I scroll through our shared music lists and find one called NYE. It looks promising. It appears to be a list of songs suitable for a New Year's Eve party: *Burning Down the House*; *L.O.V.E*; *Rocket*; *Explosions*; *We Didn't Start the Fire*; *Relight my Fire*; *Light my Fire*; *Disco Inferno*; *Sex on Fire* … The list goes on and on. How long are we meant to be performing? *We*? I'm sounding committed already.

The rest of the day is spent going through Twister's playlist, praying to God that these are the right songs and prancing around the apartment as I try to memorize lyrics. I'm nothing if not a conscientious student. Plus, the thought of looking like a complete wombat in front of Guy spurs me on.

Over and over I rehearse the damn songs. By late afternoon I'm still not convinced I'm going to pull it off. Perhaps I can explain any differences by saying I fell over because of my illness, hit my head and have mild concussion? I sing while in our crappy shower, washing my hair, brandishing my shampoo bottle. I slip into a ridiculous fantasy scenario of Guy being in there with me, serenading me on his knees …

With a mental wrench from that water-slick image, I get out. Wrapping a towel around my hair and another round my body, I check my phone for the umpteenth time. Still nothing from Twister. It looks like I'm going to have to go through with this charade. The scrap of paper lies innocently enough on the bedside table, but just a glance at the address in the suburb of St. Peter's gives me the jitters. My heart begins to patter: soon I'll be performing for Guy and goodness knows who else. I don't know whether to be terrified or thrilled. No, I'm definitely terrified.

"Strap yourself in and live a little, isn't that what you wanted?" I tell myself, gritting my teeth and smiling grimly as I apply make-up for the first time in weeks. I fix the image of Twister's facial expressions and body poses in my head. I've done this so many times, but still I practice them in the mirror. To me it looks all wrong, but perhaps it'll be good enough to fool anyone else.

Carefully applying mascara, I think back to when I last played Twister. It was well over a year ago and that had been to get her through her driving test back in the UK. I am not proud. I still feel guilty because, to be honest, Twister is a bit of liability on the road, more interested in checking her reflection in the driving mirror than checking the traffic behind her. The things I've done in the name of sisterly love are eye-watering, but they rarely keep me awake at night because, for all our disagreements and spats, at the end of the day, this is Twister we're talking about – my nearest and dearest.

Dressed and dolled up, staring at my reflection, I have a moment of panic. I wash half the make-up off again — the washed-out no-make-up look should serve me much better if Twister's supposedly not been well. I do ten minutes of meditation to calm myself, then try again.

Okay, my dark hair is a couple of inches shorter than Twister's, but it's nothing a haircut won't explain away. I'm also less curvaceous; I may have lost weight traveling or perhaps I've shrunk after too many hours spent sweating over pots and pans. There appears to be a lack of material covering my torso in Twister's barely-there-artfully-shredded white denim shorts and cropped pink t-shirt, but I can hardly go in jogging pants. I consider her five-inch heels, tossing up whether to wear those or my trainers. I'm going to need all the ammunition I can get, but the trainers win. Temporarily.

Shoving the heels into my tote bag, I grab my black trench coat thinking it will be good to cover all. Unfortunately, with the addition of the coat I now look as if I'm wearing nothing underneath — like I'm a flasher. Yikes! Tearing the coat off again, I put on my enormous sunglasses — sunglasses I bought at the start of summer, which Twister charmingly said make me look like a bluebottle fly. Tonight feels like the perfect occasion to be a fly-on-the-wall of my sister's reality show.

Dear God. I don't exactly own this look, but it'll have to do.

And now I'm running late.

Racing down the street, I conjure Twister to my mind and slow myself down to a simmering strut. She would arrive late anyway. At the back of my mind, a voice is heckling – *imposter! You're going to fall flat on your bony ass, again. Not to mention that when this is over, you're going straight to hell!*

5

The music studio is a large red brick building which looks like it's been converted from a former warehouse, faded yellow lettering high on a wall proclaiming something like *Metca ... Mortar*.

Here goes. I could do with some mortar to help keep my shit together. I surreptitiously change into Twister's heels and teeter around the corner of the street towards the entrance, focusing on not turning my ankle. *How the hell does one strut in heels?* Twister makes it look so natural but I feel like a donkey on stilts.

I press the intercom buzzer.

"Yeah?"

"It's me," I croak.

"Tilly?"

"Who else," I say, sounding more Tilly than I feel.

"You're an hour late."

"Sorry." I need to stop apologizing right now. Not Twister's style at all.

The door buzzes and I let myself in, my heart pounding faster than the drum beat I can hear thumping somewhere deep in the building. *Oh crappity crap!* I'm suddenly overwhelmed by jaw-locking nausea, my mouth salivating, my heart palpitating. *What the hell am I doing?* Leaning against the wall, I try to suck some air into my lungs.

"Tilly, you okay?" says a familiar voice.

I look over my shoulder. Backlit by the window behind him, Guy has appeared like a saintly vision silhouetted against the glass window at the end of the on the staircase. It's like trying to stare at the sun and not be blinded.

Heaven help me.

I manage to straighten up as he approaches. Good grief, he's grown even better looking since yesterday. His eyes and forehead crinkle with concern. It takes every ounce of my resolve not to fall to my knees and make a full confession.

"Do you need to sit down?" He takes my arm.

I inhale sharply, a dose of his scent — reminiscent of woodland, sparkling water, a quiet glade to lie down — snorting straight to my cortex.

"Tilly? Hello?"

His voice brings me back to my senses. "Yes. Hi. I'll be fine," I say, peeling myself free of his grasp. "I can manage."

"Come on then."

On legs like straws, I shakily follow him up the staircase clutching onto the bannister, hauling myself step by step up the staircase. The last thing I should be doing while trying to navigate a steep staircase in heels like these is be distracted by his backside, but it's right there, in my face. The denim straining taut over rippling muscle ... and those endless thighs ... strong, lean, athletic ...

At the top he turns and catches me gawping. "You sure, you're well enough for this?"

Short of breath, I drag myself the last couple of steps to the top of the stairs. Gray eyes reduce my stomach to liquid. "Of course," I lie. Actually, I could faint at any moment. Perhaps I should lie down.

His eyes narrow. "Okay. If you're sure. Same as ever, yeah?"

He seems to be waiting for my response. I nod. "Same, same," I say, desperately trying to inject some of Twister's *Whatever!* attitude into my voice.

He opens the door behind him, and we enter a large, high-ceilinged white-washed space where there are three other men chatting. From the poster I've studied, I recognize them as the other members of the band.

"Look what the cat dragged in!" Guy announces cheerfully.

I lurch over my own feet and Guy has to grab my arm again to stop me falling flat on my face. This is a totally different Guy to the one who spoke with such concern outside the room.

"Have you been fucking drinking?" he mutters under his breath, fixing me with a laser stare.

"No!" Though perhaps I should've been.

"Good." He sets me upright.

"Yo, Tilly!" says the drummer, raising his drumstick. "Dramatic entrance."

"Ha. You know me."

"She lives and walks," says the guitarist, "but can she sing?"

I rub my throat. "Hopefully I'll manage."

The saxophonist has his mouth full of saxophone, but his face creases into a smile and he winks.

They seem a friendly enough bunch, and I throw them a curtsey as well as a smile. *What am I doing? Why am I curtseying?*

"Okay, let's not waste any more time with amateur dramatics," says Guy, indicating the empty microphone next to his. "Brum, beat us in." He addresses the drummer. "When you're quite finished, Tilly."

Dumping my bag on the floor, I head for the other empty mike and clutch it in both hands. Guy picks out a tune on his guitar and the relief when I recognize it is huge. It was on Twister's Spotify list and it's also one of my favorites: *A Sky Full of Stars*.

But observing Guy out of the corner of my eye, my brain decides to shut down.

Guy raises his hand and the music skids to a stop.

"Sorry, I guess that was my cue," I say. *Bloody hell! Bloody hell! It's never been this hard being Twister before.* I close my eyes. *What would Twister do?* She wouldn't apologize for starters. I must stop doing that

— it's a dead giveaway. Twister would be more likely to make a scene. Distract. Play to whatever small audience there is to play to.

"I guess it was," drawls Guy.

"Just checking to see if you noticed. I want to know you missed me, right." I turn around and smile flirtatiously at the band.

Guy mutters something inaudible. "Okay. From the top." He starts singing. Oh man, he's amazing! Even better than I could've ever imagined. His voice sends tingles flashing across my shoulders and down my arms. For a few beats, I forget I'm there to sing again until he starts jabbing a finger repeatedly in my direction. I join in late, stumbling over the words, bumbling my way through to the last note.

"Well, that was underwhelming," says Guy at the end.

It's like a punch to the gut. His voice is mild enough, and he isn't looking at me as he says it, but I'm pretty sure we can all figure out who his comment is directed at. Being this close to Guy is like dancing with someone carrying a loaded gun. Part of me wants to run screaming from the room, but a spark of adrenaline flares deep inside me and something clears in my head. Through the fog of dread and desperation, determination pokes its head. I cannot cock this up. I will not. Not just for Twister's sake. But for the band. For Guy. And actually, I want to do this to prove something to myself.

"Maybe if we start with something a little more challenging," says Guy.

"Maybe if we start with something a little more upbeat," I counter. "What about an ABBA number?" I definitely recall Twister singing ABBA in the stairwell and they've always been family favorites. Who knows it might settle my nerves.

There's an ominous silence.

I clear my throat, jut out a hip, and take sideways glance at Guy. "Or maybe not? Stick with your plan. Whatever!" *Whatever the hell his plan is.* "Sorry I had an opinion." *Shit! Shit! No more sorries!*

I don't know Guy from Adam, but I could swear he's studying me a little too closely for comfort. "Okay. Fine. Lady's choice. *Take a chance on me,*" he says.

Relief sweeps over me. This song I can do in my sleep and,

considering the present circumstance, I might need to. I try to inject the raw, sexy quality into my voice that Twister has. I envisage her strutting her stuff in our kitchen back at home. Guy needs to take a chance on me. I need to take a chance on myself.

This time at the end, I'm rewarded with a curt nod and feel like I've been given a gold star sticker.

Unfortunately, the very next number is not one I've heard before. *Oh hell, here we go again.* Is it Australian? Was it on Twister's playlist? I look blankly at Guy.

"Tilly, you agreed to this and promised you'd have it learnt by now."

"I did learn it. But now I've forgotten it. Besides, I really hate this bloody song." *I need to turn the stroppiness up to full volume.* I fold my arms and pout.

"Fuck's sake. Let's not rehash the same old argument. Jimmy Barnes is a national icon. *Working Class Man* is practically the Australian national anthem. Yes, lads?" He turns around to get the band's back-up and they nod enthusiastically. *Traitors.* "We all agreed. We're singing it. You only need to join in for the chorus."

I shrug. "You'd better give me the lyrics then."

"What because they're so difficult to remember?" He thrusts a sheet in my direction and ungratefully I snatch it out of his hand. The chorus mostly consists of a repeat of the title.

Guy whirls his finger in the air. "Let's see if we can pick this performance up off the floor." He looks directly at me as he speaks this time and a jolt fires through me — something in his eyes tells me that's exactly where he'd like me. The image of me tussling with Guy on the floorboards is a distraction I can do without.

I mumble my way through their precious Aussie classic, images of Guy and me, legs entwined, rolling around ungracefully, filling my head.

At the end, Guy stares at me bleakly. "What's gotten into you, Tilly?"

Uh, that'd be Alice.

I'd love to tell them I'm not Twister. I know I'm doing a lousy job.

I'm more used to singing opera and leave the pop singing to Twister. I feel awkward and uncomfortable and an unmitigated disaster. It's on the tip of my tongue to tell them the truth. Staring into his unforgiving eyes, something hardens in my chest like I've swallowed a rock. "Excuse me." I march over to my handbag and take out my bottle of water.

No, you do not give up. Don't let him get under your skin. Don't be derailed just because he's horribly good looking. You *know* you can sing as well as Twister, you just chose not to. And don't you bloody dare say sorry again! "I'm parched. Whatever bug I caught has stripped my throat. Give me a bloody break, okay?"

That shuts him up. I return to my place at the front.

Despite my act of bravado, the next hour continues in much the same vein: I lose some, I win some. I drivel my way through and wreck a lot of great numbers. Guy's lukewarm response makes it only too clear what he's thinking— we're in trouble.

While he's distracted talking to the others, whose names I've by now made a mental note of — Brum on the drum, Scooter on the guitar, Fin on the sax — I flick through the music sheets on Guy's stand, desperately trying to recollect the song order and remind myself of a few lyrics.

Most of the rest of the songs I know well enough — *Firework, Feeling Good, Young Blood, Let Me Love You, I Feel it Coming, Need you Tonight, I'm on Fire* ... It definitely looks like the playlist I rehearsed earlier in the day, so that's something.

"Finished?" says Guy, in my ear.

I jump and have to grab the microphone to stop it crashing to the floor. "Yup!" I say, crossing the room to pick up my bag.

"Where do you think you're going?" Guy looks incredulous.

"You said we were finished."

"Uh, no I didn't." His expression shouts, *idiot!* "I meant have you finished messing with my stuff." Guy looks as if he wants to slap me.

I want to run from the building screaming. "God, you're so touchy this evening," I mumble.

"Touchy?"

Oh crap. "Yes. Precious."

My words dangle like fragile Christmas baubles swaying in the breeze. Only Christmas has been and gone. Why do I sense my timing and words are out of sync?

His mouth tightens. "I need a fucking break." He strides from the room.

I smile weakly at the others, and go and flop on the leather sofa at the back. "What's his problem?" I mutter. The problem is this is nuts. I must be mad to think I can pull it off. If it's bad now, what's it going to be like in front of a real audience. But, hopefully, Twister will be back before then so she can deal with it.

The rest of the band chat quietly waiting for their Lord and Master to return. I expect them to say something scathing to me, but actually they're an easy-going bunch of blokes, too busy bantering about work and girlfriends to worry. Fin beckons me over, and I go and chat. I'm just starting to feel a bit better when Guy marches back in.

"Right. *Firework*," he says. He avoids looking at me, which I guess it means he's in danger of losing control and battering someone. No prizes for guessing who. A muscle ticks away like a metronome in his sculpted jaw. He doesn't pick up his guitar this time. He plucks his microphone off its stand, closes the gap between us and starts singing the words into my face.

Are we seriously meant to be doing this number so close?

I can feel not only his breath but also the heat radiating off him. I can see the flecks of fire in his gray irises. His eyes are unflinching, staring right through me, giving me goosebumps. I barely manage to croak out the words, even though this is a song I know and love. Staring into his eyes, I flounder and then stop singing altogether. I cannot do this. He's an explosion waiting to happen. I have no problem imagining the fallout, me floating in scattered embers through the air.

Guy stops too.

"You're okay," I say, lamely.

He leans closer. "Okay is not good enough, is it? I want fireworks," he says, "not this bloody damp squib."

Wow. That's me. Not even a floaty piece of debris after an explosion. I've overestimated myself. All hope extinguished.

Something inside me pops. A bubble.

Unfortunately, or maybe fortunately, I suddenly find the whole situation hysterical. I know I must be a disappointment, and I do feel slightly sorry for him and his band because they obviously care so much about this, but ... I cannot help laughing.

I compress my lips trying to contain my mirth, but laughter snorts in an unladylike fashion from my nostrils. I clamp a hand over my mouth. The whole situation is beyond my control. Of course, I'm a damp squib compared to Twister. Hadn't that been the case our entire lives? Twister is a firecracker and I'm not even a kid's sparkler in comparison. Wave me around and you might just about fool someone you're having fun, but it doesn't take long for the magic to fizzle out. If I don't laugh at this situation, I'll cry. In fact, I want desperately to cry, but not in front of Guy. No way.

Feeling myself disintegrating, I run from the room before he notices.

6

In the bathroom, I glare at myself in the mirror. I hate myself a bit. A lot. But then I give myself a ruddy good talking to. *Stop being a wet flannel. You need to go back in there and (without apologizing!) show them what you're made of. You can sing, Alice, so bloody sing your heart out.*

There was a time in the not so distant past, when Tilly and I were teenagers, I'd loved to sing. You couldn't stop me. My parents used to praise *me* for being the one with 'the voice'. Of course, that only goaded Tilly into trying harder. She's nothing if not competitive. But to be fair, I understand that impulse to beat my other half only too well. I often feel it, but somehow, on the whole, I've managed to smother it over the years. Now here I am pretending to be Twister, wishing I was as good as her, and making a total hash of it. *But I don't want to be as good as her. I want to be better. I want to be the best. The best me at least.* I'm struggling to decide whether to come clean or not. Perhaps the band deserves to know the truth. Would that be so awful? Being Twister is so damn draining.

While I examine my poor suffering feet, I send another text to my sister.

Alice in Wanderlust

> Twister, Where the hell are you? I cannot believe I'm covering your sorry ass! AGAIN! Guy is being a total armpit. You'd better be home tonight or else! Ring me or I'll disown you. With much malice, Alice

I wait for her to respond, but it's a loser's game. A game I've played once too often lately.

Time to tell the guys the truth, and make a swift exit.

I push open the Ladies' door to find the members of the band traipsing down the stairs. "What's going on?"

"Best talk to Guy about that," says Brum waving his drum sticks and flashing a rueful smile over his shoulder. "See you tomorrow evening at the docks. Have fun in there."

Oh no. Alone with Guy. I should be elated, but instead I'm nervous as hell.

I open the door and peek in. Guy is perched on a stool staring out at the dark night and city lights beyond the glass.

"We done then?" I ask.

He spins around. Serious ramps up a few notches. "No. As much as you might wish we were, we're not. Get in here." He stands up and I let the door swing closed behind me.

"Come over here."

My heart gallops faster with every step. Blood rushes like a torrent in my head.

Guy closes the last couple of steps between us and brushes a strand of hair behind my ear. "Why didn't you come outside when I walked out earlier?" His voice is a warm caress. I shrug unable to speak. His fingers thread into my hair, cupping my head, and he draws me closer still. "You know how perfect sounds," he says, "so stop messing with me." He pauses. "Okay?"

"—kay," I croak.

For a moment I think he's going to kiss me. That would be a bit of a game changer, but it's also terrifying. He lowers his face towards mine and at the last second I panic and duck out of his grasp. My poor heart is flailing, missing its beats, flapping wildly. Wasn't I meant to be telling him the truth? Now is my chance. I grab the microphone. "No more games. Let's just sing," I squeak.

He throws me a languid smile. "Right."

"I'm happy to practice all night if need be, but not in these shoes. They're killing me." I kick one off and watch it hoop through the air missing Guy's head by millimeters.

He ducks and I totter forwards off balance. Not looking at him, I take off the other shoe more carefully, but as I toss it aside, Guy grabs my wrist.

"Are you deliberately trying to hurt me?" If looks could obliterate, I'd be a cloud of dust right now.

"No. The shoe was an accident. Sorry." *Damn it!* There I go again, being uncharacteristically apologetic. The tell-tale guilt rises unbidden to my hot cheeks and I attempt a bluff, raising an eyebrow and glaring a little, telling myself his hair is a way too scruffy anyway, and his nose a little too big, and his hooded eyes a lot too menacing for him to be classically handsome.

"What's changed?" The way his eyes roll over me up my arm to my lips, and down to my throat, leaves a wake of goosebumps. Maybe it's the air conditioning.

All of a sudden I realize Guy's eyes are transfixed, staring at the tattoo on my inner wrist.

Oh shit. Now the game really is up.

"I can explain," I whisper.

Twister and I had matching fish tattoos done on our wrists in Bali, but mine is on my left arm, while Tilly's is on the right. Put them together and they're like yin and yang. Identical, but mirror images.

I wait for him to say something. Anything.

I try to extricate my hand, but his grip tightens. His eyes rake back upwards to my blazing face. The way he stares not only at me, but inside me, convinces me my cover is blown.

I feel relieved the whole ordeal is over. Once Twister is back, I'll demand we pay our bills, hand in our notice and get back on the road … The farther away from Axel and Roger, and sadly, even Guy, the better. That last thought smarts a bit. Despite his obvious distaste for me, I've made the terrible mistake of crushing on him too much already. "What do you p—?"

Before I can ask what he plans to do, he plants his lips on mine. A thousand nerves bolt like lightning, flashing through my head, shredding my thoughts. My body surges with heat. His kiss is so unexpected and so sweet and oh, so, tender that I want to sink to the floor, taking him with me.

But the kiss stops as suddenly as it started. I realize I am still frozen to the spot.

"You were going to say?" he murmurs, brushing my hair away from my face.

Oh my God. Oh my God. Oh my God.

"Oh ..." I should look him in the face and admit the truth, but suddenly all I can think about is how I desperately want to repeat that, to feel his mouth on mine again. Our bodies are close, but I want him closer still. What must he think of me? My forehead drops to his chest and I feel the steady beat of his heart.

A lot of questions roar around in my brain that I could do with answers to. If Twister is meant to be dating Axel, why the hell is Guy kissing me? What's been going on? Why the hell hasn't Tilly said anything? She's my closest confidante, my sister, my twin, my other half for God's sake ... and I know nothing about this.

"Tilly? Look at me."

I freeze. Seriously? He still thinks I'm Twister? Now, I'm thoroughly confused. A moment ago, I thought I'd blown my cover. My thoughts numb as if someone stuck my head in a freezer. A tremor runs through me. I'm torn between telling him the truth and having what I want right here in my hands. Even as I'm thinking that, his grip loosens and his hands skim down my arms. He rests his head on top of mine.

"What do you want to do?"

Breathing would be a good start. *Inhale, exhale, inhale.*

"Have you made up your mind about us?"

Sort of. I never want this to end. I want him to want me. I groan. Oh God, maybe I need to be Twister for a bit longer.

Sucking a juddering breath into my lungs, I reply, "I ... I ... Um ... Shall we continue singing?" Perhaps I can sort out my frozen brain and everything I need to say at the same time.

"Sure." Is it my imagination or does he sound a little disappointed? "Whatever you want." He draws me over toward his music stand.

We go through the rest of the repertoire for New Year's Eve. To begin with I squawk like a parrot and expect Guy to say something, but now he's got the patience of a saint, smiling encouragingly. As time passes my confidence grows, but so does the ball of fire burning in my chest.

When we sing *Feeling Good*, his voice is like lava and his eyes smolder holes deep into my molten Nina Simone core. I take over, my voice rasping with desire and the corner of his mouth tips into a fragile smile. God I want it to stay there. I desperately want to please him. I bleed that song for all it's worth. I sing my heart out for Guy.

"Fuck me," he growls at the end. "That. That is how to sing. You're going to slay hearts tomorrow night."

I get tingles all over.

And I wait for my congratulatory kiss. My celebratory kiss? Any sort of kiss? "What's next?" I prompt.

He puffs out a breath. "You tell me." He cocks his head to one side. "You're the one calling all the shots." He traces the side of my face with the back of his hand.

I can barely breathe for anticipation.

And then he starts singing *Wicked Game*. It's haunting.

"It's time we stop with the games, don't you think?" whispers Guy at the end. His eyes are dark and penetrating.

Oh, hot holy hell. Part of me wants to weep because I suspect there is a lot more going on between Twister and Guy than with your average singing duo, and if that's the case I'm treading on sacrosanct territory. I could never do anything to hurt my sister. I'd rather die.

I unravel my fingers from his and force myself to step away. "For now, let's just get through this. The less people hurt the better," I say turning away and trying not to think about my own bruised heart.

After we finally belt out *Auld Lang Syne,* I glance at the clock on the wall and see it's gone midnight. Now we've stopped singing, an awkward silence seems to fill the space between us.

"You tired? Got any plans?" asks Guy.

"Just bed. Alone," I rasp, grasping my bottle of water and finishing it off. "Do you think I'll ... we'll be okay?"

My voice has gone all high-pitched again. Christ, I've given this my all and if I'm still not good enough. I'm not sure what's going to happen tomorrow. Personally, I thought we sounded perfect together, even though 'together' is never going to happen.

"I thought we sounded okay, didn't you? I know I'm not singing at my best and I totally understand, if you'd rather do this without me."

"No, I don't want to do this without you. We sounded better than okay and you know it. That's not what this is about."

"What's this about then?"

"You have to ask?" Studying me again, he rubs his jaw and then shakes his head as if trying to clear it.

It's time to scarper before he realizes what a fraud I really am.

"I better go." Avoiding his eyes, I screw the lid back on my bottle. I go to put on Twister's shoes again, but in the end I can't face forcing my feet into them, so I stand there, still a little undecided, bare-foot, shoes in hand. "I'll see you tomorrow at Darling Harb—"

Guy takes my hand and I drop one of the shoes. Reaching down to pick it up with my other hand, he prevents me, instead reeling me in towards his chest. "Or you could stay with me tonight." There's a challenging glint in his eyes.

Oh, how I would dearly love to say yes. This is not just temptation, this is hell. The man of my dreams is standing right in front of me and I want nothing more than to give myself to him. But there is Twister to consider.

Bitter bitter sweet, my bitter sweet twisted life.

"No, Guy, I really can't. I can't do this," I say, and tearing myself away, I run out.

7

The next morning, I wake in a sweat, the sheets tangled around my legs, feeling genuinely ill. I've hardly slept. My night has been filled with nightmares about Guy: Guy spotting my tattoo and calling my bluff in a very public way; Guy raining down punishing kisses on my lips; Guy tossing me over his shoulder and throwing me off the side of a boat; Guy tying me to a Catherine Wheel and spinning it, me lighting up Sydney as my body explodes like fireworks showering glittering shards of Alice all over the city.

"Oh God!"

If Twister isn't back soon, I don't know what I'll do. I'm not sure I can survive another night of being the great pretender, especially not at some bigwig party on board a yacht, especially not with my feelings for Guy added into the brew — and most especially not with me unable to reciprocate any feelings he may have for Twister. There is only so much temptation a girl can withstand.

I text Twister yet again.

> Twister, I'm sympathetic to a point, but this is not working out. You have to get your shit together and get your backside back here. The gig this evening is for heroes! So get your brave face on! You cannot let these people down! You need to be at Darling Harbour by 6pm. The band are all going to be wearing black-tie and Guy reminded me you need to wear the red dress. I think he means your long slinky number. It's here in the cupboard. Please reply to let me know you're alive.

I stare anxiously at my phone, but there are no scrolling dots. Unless Twister comes back soon I'm going to have to maintain this ridiculous charade because, you know, this party is for heroes, all these people who've shown incredible bravery. Letting them down would be cowardly. Surely I can summon up enough *chutzpah* to sing for one more evening.

I dash over to Axel's nightclub in case Twister might be hiding out there, but a notice on the door announces it's closed until 4th January. *You've got to be kidding! Where are they? Where is she?!*

I hammer on the door and ring the bell a dozen times. After about ten minutes, one of Axel's henchmen clad in the uniform black leather jacket, black vest and black jeans appears. "What the fuck! Axel's been hunting for you everywhere," he says, grabbing my wrist.

"Stop! Let go of me! I'm not Tilly! I'm her twin, Alice. Where his she?" I demand.

I wrench free of his grasp while the henchman scratches his balls and looks surprised. "Really? Shit man, you look exactly like her. You're not fucking with me, are you?"

"No, I'm definitely not. I need to talk to Tilly."

"Join the frigging queue. She's not here. Haven't seen her for a couple of days now."

"Where's Axel?"

"Not here either. Said he needed a break... or was it he wanted to break someone." He laughs, the shithead. "Maybe they're together ... there's a thought ... Anyway, we're closed."

"Great! That's really helpful!"

From the expression on his face, I realize it's not sensible to be venting my frustration on a six-foot-two bald-headed bouncer. Despite Twister swearing blind that she and Axel were through, I cannot help but suspect they've snuck away together for a few dirty nights of passion. I could not be more pissed off. I feel especially affronted on Guy's behalf.

My phone beeps. For about two seconds my spirits lift … until I register it's only Roger.

"If Tilly shows up, or if you hear where she is, can you ask her to contact her sister immediately, please?" I hurry away, the bouncer's eyes no doubt boring holes into my back as I scurry down the street reading Roger's text.

> Alice, where are you? You do remember you were supposed to be working today and you're late. When you come, don't forget to bring your evening gear — a cocktail dress — so we can go out straight from work. You can shower here beforehand. I have an amazing surprise lined up!

I'd forgotten to ring in sick again. Bugger. Groaning at the thought of my own supposedly 'hot' date, I text back.

> Roger, I'm so sorry, but I'm sick. I've got a disgusting bug. I can't go anywhere today, or tonight. You're going to have to find a replacement.

I watch the dots dancing.

> Jeeez Alice, I'm pissed. I sorted a special treat for you.

He adds a rocket emoji, whatever the hell that's supposed to signify.

> You sure you can't get better in time?

> I'm sure, Roger. Sick as a dog.

I add a vomit and poo emoji, pretty sure he'll be able to translate those.

> I'm sure you'll find someone else who'd love to spend the evening with you. Sadly, I can't stop ...

I spend the rest of the day muttering madly to myself, rehearsing lyrics and checking my phone. Not a word from Twister. What if there's a change of plan and Guy has to contact me? He doesn't even have my cellphone number. What if he comes around here again? I actually open the front door of the flat to check the corridor. No sign of anyone. Even so, I waste another hour vacuuming and cleaning our apartment, on the outside chance he might put in an appearance. I also put fresh sheets on the bed as an afterthought, telling myself they are due a change, but knowing my motives aren't entirely honorable.

Emotionally and mentally, I am very torn. She asked me to stand in for her, but I'm not sure she'd be too happy if she knew how I was feeling. I text her again. And again. And again. The possible reasons for her not responding run like wildfire through my overwrought brain: she could've dropped her phone in the ocean or she could be busy screwing Axel, but maybe she got so wasted she's lying in a pool of her own vomit in a gutter somewhere.

Finally, I remember phone tracker and try to locate her that way. My heart plummets: Twister's phone is not in Sydney; in fact, it's not visible anywhere in Australia — her phone is literally off the radar. What the hell does that mean?

I'm itching to call the police, but in the end the memory of her pleading for some space and a few days to sort her head prevails. It's been less than 48 hours. I'll give her until tomorrow ... although that means, unless she suddenly shows up, I'll have to sing with the band.

8

Getting out of the taxi, I scan the crowd on the quayside. I'm hoping against hope to catch sight of Twister, in which case, I can avoid this gig, but there's no sign of her. It takes me a moment to identify the band because although they're all carrying musical instruments, they're decked out in tuxedos — just when I thought Guy couldn't get any better looking ...

The beat of my heart quickens. A little self-conscious in my heels and dress, I head over.

Brum whistles and eyes turn in my direction. I feel my face coloring up nicely, pretty sure it must match the scarlet of my dress.

"You're a sight for sore eyes," murmurs Guy in my ear.

As we haul all the band equipment up the gangway, beneath the Community Hero banner and onto the vast gin palace of a yacht, I mull over his words. Did he mean he was relieved because I came, or something more? I shouldn't care, but I do. I wish I was anywhere except here, but I am almost bubbling over with excitement. Honestly, my life is like being one of Dr Doolittle's *pushmepullme* creatures.

I sternly remind myself that Guy and I are never going to be an item (at least not until I've spoken to Twister and found out exactly

Alice in Wanderlust

what the situation between them is) and to keep both my cool and my distance. Which is easier said than done, even on a boat this huge.

It's seriously impressive. Not like any boat I've ever been on before — even the balustrades and railings are ornate, sparkling with fairy lights. There are four decks in total, three for the guests and a lower deck in the guts of the boat for the kitchen and staff. On a small stage, under the shade of the white awning at the back, we set up all our kit.

I gaze around awestruck, not because of the size of the boat, but because it's so sophisticated. There's luxury and then there is this! The dance floor between us and the bar is polished to a high shine, even the leaves of the enormous plants dotted around the deck gleam.

"Fancy a snoop?" says Guy.

"Do I!"

Following him, my nerves ratchet with every step. As well as the bar on our level, there is a further bar on the deck above, comfortable seating arrayed under another awning, the striped blue cushions playing to the maritime theme, lights like stars twinkling overhead. Above that is a final viewing deck where the band are clustered, smiling nervously at one another, assessing which person is looking the most terrified. I win hands down.

One of the crew appears with a tray of drinks. "On the house. Or boat, I should say." He laughs. "To wet your whistles. Hope it's a great night!"

I gulp the glass of wine down like water. To avoid looking at my hands, I focus on the view of Sydney. Brum, Fin and Scooter wander off again and I'm left with Guy.

"You learn all the lyrics yet?" he asks leaning next to me on the railing.

"Think so." The water churning below is nothing compared to my stomach. "Do you think … um … there'll be many people tonight?"

"Standing room only. I believe the captain mentioned a couple of hundred, something like that."

"Shit a brick!"

He glances sideways at me. "Nervous?"

Crapping myself. "A little. You?" My hands are shaking so violently, I'm in danger of spilling my wine. He places a finger on my wrist as if to gauge my pulse, or perhaps steady me, I'm not certain which.

"Don't worry," he says. "Once we get singing, you'll be sensational."

"That's not the impression you gave me last night."

"Yeah, well, I was confused. About you. About everything. I have your shoe by the way. You left it behind, Cinderella." A smile curves his beautiful mouth upwards, as he looks down at my feet. Perhaps he's expecting to see glass slippers — or the cloven hooves of a she-devil. I'm struck again by how exquisitely handsome he is, the breeze ruffling his dark hair, his gray eyes glittering like the sea reflecting the golden evening.

Oh, bloody hell. Perhaps I should throw myself overboard already.

With an effort I pull myself together and try to crack a joke. "A shoe does not a Prince Charming make," I say, "and believe me, I'm no Cinderella." I grit my teeth. Do he and Twister have something going on or don't they? I have to find out. He's not the only one confused after last night.

"Yeah, well, I'd *like* to say you don't have anything to worry about, Cinders, but I'm not so sure."

"Why? D-do you think I'm going to turn into a pumpkin. M-make a tit of myself?"

"A tit?" he laughs, and his eyes stray towards my cleavage. "You're … perfect." He swallows and stares out across the water. "But perhaps that dress was not such a smart idea."

"You *told* me to wear this! What's wrong with it?"

He hesitates. "Everything."

'Well, thanks a bunch. It's a bit bloody late to change now."

"Way too late." He takes a gulp of his beer and leans so close I can smell the stomach-warming scent of him. His words whisper in my ear, "How the hell do you expect me to sing or keep my hands to myself looking like you do?"

I look up at him, not believing I've heard straight. He stares back, his eyes liquid and deeper than the water below. My mind goes blank and I clutch my glass tighter. *I think he said he likes my dress ... or me ... but his face is a blank mask, and I probably misheard. Am I inappropriately dressed?* I open my mouth to ask and close it again. *I can't think of anything to say because all I want to do is kiss him ... but I can't.*

Like him, I stare fixedly at the sea.

After a moment, he gives me a gentle nudge. "Don't worry about me. I'll endeavor to keep my hands to myself. Besides, if you sing anything like you sang last night, I imagine I'll be too busy fighting off your dozens of admirers with my microphone."

I smile at the thought. "You said I was underwhelming." I know I'm fishing, but I want to hear him say more nice things about me, so I can be certain I heard him correctly before.

"Maybe to begin with. You certainly sounded different. But then ... it's not surprising you sounded so awkward ... as you'd never sung with us before."

"What?" My heart lurches over the side of the boat. I grab hold of the rail to steady myself. The rumble of the engine vibrates up through my legs and I tremble. "How ... when did you ...?"

"Realize you're not Tilly?" It isn't an accusation, or a question, so much as a statement. "I couldn't put my finger on it last night until I spotted your tattoo. Wrong wrist." He smiles ruefully. "You had us all fooled. Even me."

The wind whips my hair over my face and I'm thankful for the screen between us. He takes my hand and gently turns it over, kissing my tattoo.

"So, when you k-k-kissed me ... before ... you kn-knew I wasn't Tilly?" I ask, brushing my hair away and studying him.

"Guilty as charged. Tilly's tattoo is on her right wrist and yours in on your left. You hold the mike with your left hand too. And your wine glass. I'm guessing you're left-handed, unlike Tilly. When you smile, you have a dimple that side as well." He touches my cheek. "Tilly's is on her right cheek. You're like mirror images of one another. The same and yet... totally different."

Oh my God. When he kissed me last night he knew I wasn't

Twister. That's confusing. That changes everything…I think. "This is not Tilly's fault. She needed some time. She's got a lot going on right now … Are you angry with me?"

"Furious." He smiles. He doesn't look furious at all. He looks as if he's teasing.

"Do you know where Tilly is?" I croak.

His face becomes serious. "If I knew where she was, we wouldn't be having this conversation." He pauses. "You don't?"

"She hasn't been answering my calls or texts. She said she needed a few days to get her head straight. Do you know why? Was it because of you?"

He looks away and exhales wearily. "Possibly. But not how you think. Not how Axel thought either. He threatened to break my legs, and although I think and hope he was bluffing, it may have spooked your sister."

"He what? Oh my God. That bloody meathead! If he's threatened Tilly, if he's touched a hair on her head, I'll … I'll rip his bloody balls off."

"She may like having her hair touched." He brushes a strand of mine aside. "For a hot second there I thought it was me you wanted to defend."

I can't help smiling. "I hope she hasn't gone back to him."

"Yeah, me too. As her *friend*."

"What the hell should I do?" I look at my phone as if a message might miraculously have appeared.

"When did you last see her?"

"She was there when you came to the flat the other day. Sorry, I lied. It wasn't because of you specifically, but she didn't want to talk to anyone. She was upset. She begged me to give her some time out. Some space to figure out stuff."

He nods as if he expected it. "Give her space then, if that's what she wants. Look if she's not home by tomorrow, I'll help you hunt her down."

"And what about this whole scene," I say, gesticulating miserably at myself and the boat.

His smile broadens. "What about it? Do what you do best. Sing your heart out and pretend to be your sister."

I gulp. "That is not what I do best. But I might need another drink. Dutch courage and all that. When Twister reappears, I'm going to bloody crucify her." For all my brave words, my voice quavers unhappily.

"Join the queue. You and me both."

Side by side, we walk down the steps to the deck below and I do my best to ignore the sparks that flash through me when his sleeve brushes my bare arm. *Honestly, I need to toughen up. Work on my immunity. It's only a sleeve.*

"So, you're obviously her twin," says Guy at the bottom of the steps, "but I still don't know your name."

"Alice. Pleased to meet you." I hold out my hand pretending to be all businesslike.

He takes it and doesn't let go. "Well, Alice. It's been an unexpected pleasure getting to know you. I'm so looking forward to your performance this evening."

What performance exactly is he talking about? Tendrils of fire flicker to my core. "You sure you still okay with me singing in Tilly's place?"

"More than ever."

My skin tingles. "I'm no Tilly."

"I'm well aware of that. You're Alice. My hero. Heroine. My singing diva."

My insides are awash with lust again. "Oh, shut up!" I laugh.

He wraps an arm around my shoulders as we head down to the next level. "If you get nervous, imagine you're singing for just one person. Whoever that special person may be. I find it helps me. You ready?"

To my horror I see passengers coming on board. "As I'll ever be."

9

*G*uy takes my hand and leads me onto the stage. The others are there, already warming up. Guy runs us through the order of play for the first set, and I half-listen while my eyes stray to the guests filtering onto the boat. There's a lot of bling and sequins. Loads of laughter and chatter. Smothering my frayed nerves, I step up to the microphone. I close my eyes and try to channel my inner diva.

We start off light with *Something just like this* and then roll straight into *Holding out for a hero*. The music choice is perfect for a night all about heroes. The deck swells with guests, the chink of glasses and the babbling of excited voices. It's difficult to imagine the boat staying afloat with this many people.

Not much later, the boat pulls away from the quayside and we launch into *Superman*. I wonder if I've found my own superhero though Guy looks nothing like Clarke Kent. We are killing the song (in a good way) and we've got these confident smiles plastered across our faces, and every time I catch Guy's eyes, it sparks a little firework inside me, giving me the warm fuzzies which just keep spreading.

All is going swimmingly well until the middle of the fifth song. I spot someone at the bar who makes me stumble over my words and, *oh my God*, he's staring directly at me as if he wants not only to make me trip up, but toss me overboard as well. He's the last person in Sydney I want to see — Roger.

Bearded and scowling, for once he looks a bit like Blackbeard – at least Blackbeard's flakey brother, wearing black leather trousers and a flouncy white silk shirt, open to his waist to show off a medallion nestled in a sea of black chest hair.

I limp through the rest of the song, fixing my eyes on Guy, who seems to have registered the fact that I might be about to throw up. Out of the corner of my eye, I see Roger weaving his way through the throng of people towards the stage. Arms folded, he takes up position right in front of me.

I do the only thing I possibly can do in the circumstances – pretend I don't know him.

At the end of the song, he barks my name. "Oy, Alice!"

Guy's eyes narrow. I smile apologetically to both him and Roger, doing my best to look confused instead of mortified.

"Fancy meeting you here!" says Roger.

"Sorry? Are you talking to me?" I ask in a small voice.

"Yes, I'm talking to you! You said you were sick."

I give an insincere laugh. "Sorry? I don't know you, do I?" Before throwing a pleading look at Guy

"Course you fucking know me. I'm your boss."

"Celebrity status already, Tilly?" says Guy stepping forward and putting a protective arm around my shoulders. "Sorry, mate. No autographs just yet."

"I don't want an autograph, you moron. I want to know what Alice is doing here when she should've been on a date here, but with me. Here." He looks like he's beginning to confuse himself.

Guy steps down off the podium. He is taller than Roger, but not so thickset in the shoulders – or head.

"Mate, I think this is a case of mistaken identity. This is Tilly. She sings with us. Everyone in the band will vouch for her. I've no idea who your Alice is, or where she is, but we've some entertaining to get on with. Tilly, you ready?" Turning his back on Roger, he steps back onto the stage looking totally cool and starts strumming his guitar.

Oh yes, I've definitely found my hero for the night.

"Sure am," I say said. My voice is shaky for the next number. Roger doesn't move. He eyeballs me the whole way through the song.

"Got yourself a groupie," mutters Guy under his breath.

I sing on, I'd like to say valiantly, but it's difficult to lift the mood when faced with Roger looking so unjolly. The situation is made worse when another face I recognize, Kylie, the waitress of ladies' toilet infamy, makes her way through the crowd to join him. What is this? A pirates' convention?

"Hey, it's Alice," she shouts, clinging onto Roger's arm and giving me a friendly wave.

"Yeah, don't I know it."

The song ends and Kylie claps enthusiastically. "Brilliant, Alice. You're amazing!"

Embarrassed, I smile, but I have to ignore her too, which feels properly rude. If I make it through tonight alive, I swear I'm never *never* going to pretend to be Twister again.

"Come on, Rog, I want that drink," says Kylie after a couple more songs, hauling him away.

I somehow make it through the next half an hour, trying to ignore the fact I'm trapped on a boat with my nemesis. I spend a lot of time staring desperately into Guy's eyes as if he were the life raft that might stop me from drowning. To give him his credit, Guy holds everything together and the band performs brilliantly.

Finally, Guy announces it's time for a break. I sprint towards the entrance for the lower deck, but as I grab the handle of the door labelled 'Crew Only' another hairy hand slaps on the door in front of my face, closing it.

"Where're you scampering off to, Alice?"

I turn around to find Roger. He hooks a fat finger through one of the shoelace straps of my dress and pulls me towards him. "Caught red-handed, my love. You're in so much trouble."

"Was my singing that bad?" At first I try to laugh it off, looking around desperately for some support, but Guy's busy talking to a well-heeled matron in a glittery black dress. I remind myself tonight is all about heroes and being brave, and despite the fact that my legs feel like jelly, I too have a backbone, and it's about time I showed it. "Get your hands off me before I report you."

"My hands aren't on you." Roger gives the strap of my dress a sharp tug and it breaks. Gasping, I clutch the material as it sags, fumbling to hold my dress up and feeling dangerously close to tears.

"How bloody dare you?"

"Oh, you haven't seen anything yet, doll," he says, sneering. "I dare do far worse than that." He's talking quietly, leaning over me with his garlicky breath, one hand still preventing me from opening the door and making my escape.

"I don't doubt it, but what do you think is going to happen when I scream? And don't for one second doubt that I will. Now move."

A brisk wind seems to pick up from nowhere. The boat rocks and Roger lurches, forced to grab onto the railing for support.

I hold my ground. "I've no idea who you are, but you're obviously confusing me with my twin sister. We're identical. People often muddle us up. Alice wouldn't have been able to go anywhere tonight though as she's sick at home."

His piggy eyes narrow and he tugs on his beard. "Oh so now you admit to Alice. But the problem is, I'm not stupid. I don't believe you're a twin."

"To be honest, I don't really give a shit what you believe, or why I should prove it," I say putting on my best swagger. "However, as in the spirit of this evening ... " Holding my dress up with one hand, I rifle through my handbag with the other, pulling out my purse. "I'll prove it."

With some difficulty, I open the purse clasp and show him the photo of my family. "See. That's me, Tilly, and that's Alice. And that's my mum and dad. And that's our brother, Harry." God, now I'm also feeling homesick to add to my woes. I wish Harry were here. He'd have frightened the bejeezus out of Roger.

"That could be a fake photo."

"What? So, you think I've just magicked this photo out of thin air? We're here to provide the music tonight, not the tricks."

Roger goes to grab my purse.

"Don't touch it!" I hiss.

He puts his hands up as if in surrender. "So what was your name again?"

"Tilly," says Guy, placing a hand on my shoulder, "I was just coming to find you. Let's go get a drink."

"I'm Tilly," I reiterate.

"Look mate," says Guy, "if you have a problem with anyone in our band, Tilly included, you talk to me."

"I think she's a liar," says Roger puffing out his chest.

"Well, bully for you. I don't know how many people you've bribed to get yourself a ticket on board here tonight, but you're clearly no hero." Guy pokes him in the chest and Roger deflates a little. "If you so much as come within spitting distance of Tilly again, I'll personally throw you overboard. You could be the owner of this fucking vessel for all I care. Is that clear enough?"

I'm gobsmacked. I've never wanted to throw my arms around anyone more or cheer louder. I settle for wrapping the arm that isn't holding up my dress about his waist.

"Hmmmphh. We'll see about that," Roger says, turning around and heading towards a hovering Kylie.

"Easy mistake to make, Rog. I thought she was Alice too. Peas in a frickin' pod," I hear her say.

In the Crew Only quarters, Guy holds up a safety pin. "Look what I've procured. Turn around."

I turn my back to the room.

Cool hands undo the zip at the back of my dress. I can't help trembling.

"Sorry, I know I promised not to touch you, but this is an exception, right?"

"Absolutely ... I don't mind ..."

His hands still.

Wrong. Wrong. Wrong. I should mind.

"Sorry. That's not what I meant. It came out wrong," I say.

"Still ... interesting." He continues hooking the strap of my dress through the safety pin and securing it to the main fabric. He zips me up again. He's pretty damn adept with his hands, not that I should even about think that, but his touch leaves me fizzing, inside and out, like a mannequin that's been brought to life but doesn't know how the hell to act human.

Placing his hands on my hips, he turns me around to face him again.

I suspect my face must be burning red with shame and lust.

"If we weren't here on this boat, right now, I'd peel this damn dress off," says Guy, a muscle twitching in his jaw. "You're more trouble than Tilly. You know that?"

Finally, I get to beat my sister at something. "Sshhh! Someone might overhear you."

"Come on. I think you need some fresh air. You're looking green." He hooks a friendly arm through mine and leads me upstairs again. He's right. The sea air is like a salve for my very hot head. It's easy for us to find a quiet spot because the guests are busy listening to speeches. Guy steers me up another two levels to the topmost deck. "We've got at least quarter of an hour before we're needed again."

The beautiful lights of Sydney look more sparkly than ever.

"You going to be okay for our next half?" he asks looking worried.

"What could possibly go wrong?"

"Well, the boat might sink for starters."

"Don't even suggest that!" I laugh, punching his arm.

"Ow." He rubs it, grinning.

"Holy mackerel. Isn't this beautiful?" I fix my sights on the twinkling lights along the shoreline, the water rippling like black silk below us.

"So very beautiful," says Guy.

Somehow he's maneuvered himself behind me so I'm caged

between his arms, but it feels like the perfect place to be, and I can't help but lean back against his chest, reminded of the scene from Titanic. If the boat were to sink now, I'd die happy. "Thank you for stepping in with Roger, but I think I had it covered."

"Of course, you did. I'm sure one-handed karate is your forté. You do know the jerk then?"

"He's my boss."

"What a meathead! Was it true that you were supposed to be out on a date with him tonight?" Guy's cheek brushes against mine making my entire body tingle.

"Not exactly. He asked, but I hadn't said yes. He seemed to have jumped to the wrong conclusion. I need to get better at saying no. That's going to be my New Year's resolution."

"Don't be over hasty." A low laugh rumbles out of him as he rests his chin on my shoulder. "You might break my heart if you say no to me."

The engine and noise from downstairs are thrumming inside me. A roar of applause drifts up from below.

"It depends, of course, what you're asking," I say, barely able get the words out. I want this so much. I want *him* so much.

"For starters, how about, can I kiss you again?"

His lips touch my bare shoulder. It's a whisper of a kiss but it reduces my insides to rubble.

Yes. Yes please. "Please don't," I moan. "I've got to make it until the end of the evening without disintegrating."

10

The second half of the evening is easier than the first because Roger makes himself scarce – with any luck he's fallen overboard. My fingers stray to my shoulder, to the broken strap of my dress Guy helped me to fix, to the spot Guy kissed afterward. I feel as if part of me is dancing on air like a spark from a bonfire, drifting and dancing into the night.

As far as our singing together goes, everything seems to fall into place and the two of us match each other in perfect harmony. There's a whole lot of eye-gazing and non-verbal communication, and some definite magic happening aboard tonight. The atmosphere is charged and full of promise, and I wonder if it is just me or if anyone else aboard is feeling the same way.

On the dance floor, bodies collide and unite and spin, a celestial microcosm of its own making. I hadn't noticed until now quite how intense the songs we've chosen are. Numbers like, *The Sweetest Taboo, Pull up to the Bumper, Sledgehammer* and *I Can't Get No Satisfaction*. The words swell with significance especially when Guy sings, this time with a sardonic eyebrow raised, looking directly into my eyes and ignoring his audience.

I've never felt sexier, nor more aroused, nor more powerful. I suspect I'm intoxicated by the potent atmosphere on the boat. Everything about Guy, every little look or touch sends hot shivers surging through my body like shots of adrenaline; singing with him is like riding a wave. He's addictive. It would take a much stronger woman than me not to smile back when he smiles, not to lean in closer when he leans towards me, not to be locked in his loaded gaze when his eyes hold mine.

It's all an act, I remind myself. All a performance.

There's a pause in the music for the midnight countdown and fireworks.

"You okay?" asks Guy handing me a glass of champagne he's magically summoned up out of nowhere. He wraps an arm around my shoulders again and, as we head towards the edge of the deck to get a better view, his fingers drift across my skin sending fireflies darting through me again.

Even watching the silhouetted forms of the many guests, hearing their excited gasps and shouts and laughter, I still feel like the two of us could be the last two people on earth. Inside I'm lit up, phosphorescent, luminous with desire. I'm also acutely, agonizingly aware of him. His every breath. His every move. The heat of his arm. His eyes reflecting the glowing lights.

The night is laced with the scent of alcohol, gunpowder and smoke, and it feels dangerous.

Real firecrackers explode making me jump. Laughing softly, both of Guy's arms close around me and our breaths mingle. Face to face, Guy's hand trails down my spine toward the center of my bare back and he presses me closer still.

Around us people start to shout, counting down to New Year's Eve.

"Ten!"

Guy runs the back of his hand down my cheek.

"Nine!"

Guy lifts my chin.

"Eight!"

His thumb brushes over my lips.

"Seven!"

I stare up into his liquid eyes, mesmerized.

"Six!"

A soft smile plays on his mouth.

"Five!"

He cups my face between both his hands.

"Four!"

He lowers his head.

"Three!"

"Before you make any daft resolutions," he murmurs.

"Two!"

He kisses me.

"One!"

Fireworks explode and the night erupts with universal cheers. I feel his smiling lips on top of mine.

He pulls back a fraction, staring into my eyes. "Happy New Year, Alice," he whispers.

"Happy New Year, Guy," I croak.

A fountain of jeweled colors – diamond, amethyst, emerald – shoots up toward the inky sky, glittering and cascading in a rain of light back toward the earth.

"They're amazing, aren't they?" I say, heat stealing into my cheeks as I look at the fireworks.

"You are." I don't need to turn my head back to him to know he's looking at me and not the sky.

"Oy, lovebirds. Can you break it up for *Auld Lang Syne?*" Brum shouts across the deck.

Laughing, hand in hand, we resume our positions on the stage and the music starts again.

"Should auld acquaintance be forgot and never brought to mind, should auld acquaintance be forgot and auld lang syne ..." I have no idea what I'm singing about any more. I'm tearful and delirious, my head buzzing and my heart stomping as I fight my euphoria. Fireworks continue to shower the night sky and, when Guy touches my hand, my own riot of sparks course inside.

At the end of the song, everyone on the dance floor seems to fall into one another's arms again, kissing and hugging. I feel suddenly shy. We sing a couple more numbers and then Guy calls it a night. Recorded music comes on and we begin to pack up. We're thanked and praised, and I glow with pride and relief, but I'm also splintering inside. What about us? What about Twister? What now?

Roger stumbles over. "You can tell your shitter, Alice, she's not sacked. I've made a resolution to be nisher to everybody. Not her fault she's sick. An' sorry about your dress. Though … looks great." He squints and grins – jolly plastered.

"I'll pass on your message," I say and watch him stagger away towed by Kylie. Thinking of messages, I'd better get hold of Twister. This not-knowing situation is killing me, not to mention the fact that this is the first New Year's Eve I can remember when I haven't been at her side. Suddenly I miss all my family like crazy.

Guy disappears to talk to a member of the boat's staff. I grab my handbag and take my phone out, just as it buzzes. And I light up when I see it's Twister at last!

Threading my way through the disembarking crowd, I rush to the quiet side of the boat and swipe open the message.

> Happy New Year Malice! Forgive me for running off and sorry I haven't replied to any of your messages – I've been in the air.

She what?

> By now you'll be celebrating New Year's Eve, hopefully on the boat with the lads, but I've a few hours to go yet cos … I'm in the UK so behind you time wise! I just landed at Heathrow. Yes, I know. Not planned. Don't kill me. I decided to come home.

WTF Twister! I read on in a growing state of shock.

> I thought if I told you, you'd dissuade me, or worse – insist on coming with me! I don't want to ruin your dreams and adventures, Alice. You have to keep going. We'll hook up again at some point soon, just not in Australia.
>
> Love you always and forever.
>
> Happy New Year!
>
> Tilly xx

"No way! You cannot have gone back to England without telling me," I whimper, and start frantically texting back.

> Happy New Year, but WTF Twister! I can't believe you'd leave without me! Why? FFS!

Hearing Guy's voice, I glance over my shoulder. He's talking to Scooter, Brum and Fin. Looking at the remaining guests, milling around, I think it'll be a while before we can make our escape.

Twister replies:

> It's complicated

I'll give her complicated!

> You've said that before. I don't care! I need to know what's going on.

I need to know if there is anything serious between Guy and Twister. Is he the reason she left?

> Twister, I have to know what the deal is with you and Guy! Did something happen between you two? Is that why you and Axel broke up? Is that why you left?

I stare at my phone, willing Twister to hurry up and respond. *Come on, come on!* The dots scroll and scroll and scroll. What is she texting, an essay?

A hand on my shoulder makes me jump.

"There you are," says Guy. "I thought you'd done a Cinderella on me again."

I half turn, my head in a spin, my eyes distracted by utterly divine Guy, slightly tired and disheveled, his bowtie hanging loose around his neck now, his collar undone. And my fingers fumble over my cellphone. My focus whips back to my hand, and I scrabble to keep hold of it, but my phone slips through my fingers.

"Oh shit!"

My cellphone tumbles head over tail, spinning through the air, before plunging into the dark water below with a soft splosh …

"Oh man! Was that…?" Guy leans over the railing.

"My phone. Oh bugger! Bugger, bugger, bugger!"

Biting his lip to stop himself from laughing, he pulls me into his arms, hugging me tight. "Oh fuck, Alice, I'm sorry. I hope that wasn't my fault. Please tell me you have everything backed up."

"That's not the point." I am momentarily distracted, and comforted, because who needs a phone when they have Guy's arms wrapped around them?

"With the money we've earned tonight I can buy you a new phone," he murmurs into my hair. "Christ, I'll get you anything you want."

I pull away so I can gauge his expression and check if he's for real.

His eyes are darker than the sky above, specks of light glittering mischievously in their depths.

"I don't want you to get me anything. I'm such a klutz. Always have been. It was my fault. Besides, I couldn't accept—"

My words are swallowed by warm lips. He tastes of champagne.

"What couldn't you accept?" he whispers, kissing me again. "This?" And he kisses me again. "Or this?" He nips my ear lobe. "Me?"

I'm slain, unable to move, intoxicated.

Tender and tentative, his lips explore, and before I know what I'm even thinking, my fingers have threaded into his soft, silken hair and I'm kissing him back without restraint. After an evening of lusting from a safe distance, suddenly I can't get close enough. My body arches against his and his hands press me closer still.

"I only have one resolution for the new year," he growls in my ear, kissing my neck, grazing the flesh with his teeth.

"What's that?" I gasp, clutching on to him for support.

"No more games. I take you home and make you mine," he says. "Would you accept that? Or is your New Year's Resolution seriously to keep saying no."

For a fraction of a second I consider. I'm sure if there was anything going on between him and Twister, he'd tell me, but his face looks so earnest and open and trustworthy, and his words are not so much a request as an invitation. My own golden ticket.

"I've adapted my New Year's resolution somewhat," I say shakily.

"Oh yes?" He smoothes my hair away from my forehead, making me tingle and shiver some more. "Tell me."

To be me. "One. Not to pretend to be Tilly ever again."

"Very wise."

"To live a little."

"How about to live a lot?"

"To live a lot. That sounds even better."

"Anything else?"

"I wouldn't object to one more kiss ..."

"Only one?" His lips smile against mine as he kisses me again.

I melt into his embrace thinking, what could be a better way to start the new year than with love and fireworks? This isn't just the first day of the year, it's the first day of the rest of my life ...

The End

Want to find out what happens between Alice and Guy? The sequel, 'Alice and the Impossible Game' is coming very soon (1st February 2024). You can grab it for a preorder bargain price now:
My Book

BONUS SCENE FROM ALICE AND THE IMPOSSIBLE GAME

Attempting to walk like you're sober as a nun while feeling giddy with lust is, quite frankly, impossible. I steal a sideways glance, forget to breathe altogether and stumble over my own feet.

Muffling a laugh, Guy steadies me with a hand on my arm.

"Hold on." I pause to take off my heels. This is unreal. He's surreal. It's the first hour, of the first day of a brand new year and , shoes in hand, I'm feeling properly footloose and fancy-free, like Im walking on air rather than the grimy Sydney sidewalk.

On impulse, I turn to Guy. "Can I ask you a question?"

A smile plays at the corner of Guy's mouth. "That was a question."

"Okay, smart-ass. Can I ask a more meaningful question? And don't tell me that was a question too."

He smirks. "Ask away."

I resist the temptation to roll my eyes. "What do you think of me? Be honest."

He laughs. "I think you like to ask loaded questions. How would you feel about being put on the spot like that?"

This, apart from all his other more obvious physical attributes—a contradiction of imposing height, expressive eyebrows, fencepost jawline, molten eyes and soft beguiling mouth—is what I like about

Guy. He's no fool, and he's clearly not just a tormented musician with the morals of an alley cat and a gravelly voice that makes every woman within earshot want to tear off her clothes. Myself included.

He is awesome...and then some.

Quite possibly a different species.

I bite down on my mounting excitement.

To be honest, I've had more than a couple of glasses of champagne and that, coupled with his challenging, come-hither expression, go some way to explaining my light-headedness. Or maybe it's just my blood not getting where it needs to — like my brain.

Tonight is like I've stepped into an old Hollywood movie, all sepia tones and fuzzy focus, the backdrop distant music, laughter and fireworks. Sydney at showtime. Australia looking magical and mysterious, windowpanes silvered, the air a warm caress, a whiff of gun smoke lingering.

"So, what d'you think of *me*?" he asks.

Beneath my bare feet, the pavement shifts from dark to amber with every streetlight. Guy and I separate like streams diverging either side of a lamppost, before coming together again. The back of his hand brushes mine and heat surges up my arm as if I've been hot-wired.

"Um...I'd say...uh...you're magic?"

"Magic?" He mimics my Yorkshire accent and hooks his fingertips beneath mine, drawing me closer. His voice is caress. "Does that mean you're under my spell?"

Absobloodylutely.

Lava courses through my veins. His lips are so close and yet so far. He raises the one eyebrow, waiting for my answer.

"Yes, um...No, of course not!" I lie. "I mean, you're great an' all, don't get me wrong. I'm in awe of your musical talent. But I'm no gropey. *Groupie*!" Holy crap, my clodhopping tongue! There's some weird voodoo zapping through the streets tonight. No wonder I'm unravelling.

We walk on some more.

"Why are you so quiet?" he asks.

I'm quiet because this feels momentous. A big decision. Epic. Me trying to decide whether to act on my feelings or not is like watching the longest tennis rally ever playing out in my head. *To be or not to be or to be maybe or maybe not...*Not to mention that physically I'm combusting, burning up, caught in the bushfire between desire and concern. Is this the right thing to do? Thoughts of my sister flit like bats in the dark.

"Nowt. Just thinking," I croak, attempting indifference. "IS your place much farther?"

"Not far. Not getting cold feet, are you?" he asks.

Yes and, of course, no. "Dirty feet, more like."

His laughter is a warm, appreciative rumble.

God, I'm bloody hilarious. In my head, at least. Tonight, I could give Twister—that's my identical twin sister, Tilly—a run for her money.

"Dirty, I approve of," says Guy, reeling me into his arms. He pauses to cup my face between his palms before kissing me soundly on the lips.

Oh. Dear. God.

This meltdown isn't normal, is it? This isn't some tonsil-tackling wrangle behind the bike sheds at school or while squished into a dank passageway at the side of the Pickled Inn in Little Pickering. Home seems a long way away. Another galaxy.

Guy's kiss is startling and languid in equal measure. He's reassured. Confident. Beguiling. Everything I am not. I want to latch on to him limpet-fashion to stop myself being consumed by the volcano, and of course Twister's advice—*Play it cool*—repeats like a persistent ringtone in my head. *Play it cool. Play it cool. Play it cool.*

Cool is not possible when my brain is sloshing around crotch-level.

Honest to God, my knees are buckling. Kissing Guy is hitting every sweet spot. While my insides slide south, my hands clutch at fistfuls of his shirt breathing in his laughter as he walks me steadily backward toward a brick wall.

Wedged between the wall and Guy, a voice whines in my head

like a damn mosquito. *Oh, come on, Alice, you cannot be serious. Not here. Not like this!*

But I want this. I want exactly this. Guy is not only the best aphrodisiac, he's the best analgesic. No more sensible, strait-laced Alice. No, Alice, Twister's awkward sister. No Alice McMalice.

Not tonight.

I swat romance-sabotaging Alice McMalice thoughts aside.

Tonight, tonight, won't be just any other night. Tonight, I'm possessed by another woman—a sexy, lustful, out-of-control trollop. Like Twister on steroids. If she can abandon me and jump on a plane back to England without explanation, I'm sure I can abandon my inhibitions and worries about her and her feelings for one evening and focus on Guy and his beautiful cheekbones and whatever other bones he may possess...

Classy! goes McMalice. *You're going to pop your cherry up against a brick wall next to some reeking garbage bins in a fugue of rotten cabbage? How romantic. I suppose it'll be memorable, if nothing else.*

I tear my lips from Guy's. "Wait!" Taking a page from Twister's book, I throw him a heated glance from beneath my eyelashes.

Guy's fingers brush across my collarbone, making me tremble. "You're right."

Am I? Letting go of my inhibitions is also good, right? It's about bloody time. I want to be free and easy. If the world is my oyster, I am its shiny pearl. In front of me is my very own rock star, guitar slung across his shoulders, his smile an irresistible magnetic force. Why shouldn't I throw caution to the wind, dance down the street and twirl around lampposts? It's time I put my past firmly in the past.

But Guy has taken hold of my hand and is now dragging me along in his wake, racing us both along the street.

"Slow down!" I gasp, gurgling with laughter. I try to match his long strides, but I'm not much of a runner. It's encouraging to see he wants this—whatever *this* is—as much as I do.

"My place is just around the corner. Keep up!" He grins back at me, slowing only a fraction.

It's like coasting on water, surfing on a wave of passion that's carrying me onwards and upwards. I want to rejoice. Tonight is the first night of the rest of my life. I'm finally stepping out of Twister's twilight, being myself. Tonight, I can be anyone I want to be. I can be sexy diva, sex goddess, sex kitten, a sex machine...

My legs pound the pavement, my lungs scream for air. *Tonight, tonight, won't just be—*

"Ow! Ow! Ow! Shit, stop!" I yell, yanking my hand from his and hopping about on one foot. "Hell's bells, my bloody foot!" I wobble around, profanities blistering my lips, still clinging on to Guy's hand while trying to peer at the sole of my foot—not easy when the lighting is dim and my vision obscured by tears of pain.

"What is it?" Guy bends and squints as well.

My foot is black with grime.

"I must've stepped on something. Ow, bleeding' heck. Oh my... my...fornicating foot!"

Guy chuckles. "Your fornicating foot?"

It's the vicar's daughter coming out in me. "Okay my *fucking* foot!"

"Steady on." Unexpectedly, he scoops me up into his arms.

Is he for real? "Don't be soft! Put me down, you nutter!"

Or maybe don't. This is rather nice being carried along with my arms looped around his neck. I bury my face in his neck and inhale. God he smells great. Like warm sun and exotic spice. "How far d'you think you can carry me like this?"

"S'not...that far...just round...the corner." He staggers bravely on a few more steps before putting me down.

As he opens a wrought-iron gate, I sympathize with the protesting hinges, but the terraced house in front of me is a good distraction. It is enchanting. Pink bougainvillea trailing along the wall and front porch, a bijoux front garden, wrought-iron balustrades on the second floor —I'm already visualizing a scene from Romeo and Juliet—a terrace out front with two deck chairs. Very quaint.

"You live here? But it's so...so charming!"

"What were you expecting, a dump?"

"Ha, no! I don't know. Certainly not this." I can't keep the smile from my lips.

The image of the two of us in fifty years' time sitting on those deck chairs, champagne flutes in hand, watching the world go by, flashes through my head before being quickly dispelled by his arm around my waist, urging me up the garden path to his cherry red front door.

"How am I meant to resist you when you're this gorgeous," he growls in my ear propping me up against the door.

My breath hitches as he trails kisses down my neck to my shoulder.

Me, gorgeous? I could get used to being called that. *Tonight, I'm the goddess of gorgeous*, I try to reassure myself. I clutch fistfuls of his T-shirt as the door swings open behind me. Laughing, Guy gathers me up in his arms again and lifts me over the threshold.

Church bells chime in my head. *Ding! Dong!* "I didn't have you pegged as a romantic."

"Ah, but you don't know me very well. Yet..."

Ay, but I will soon. Every sexy inch.

Still carrying me, Guy staggers along the hallway, flicking on a light switch with his elbow while I send a football flying from the hall table with my foot. It bounces noisily across the floorboards as we pinball together along the passageway, down a couple of steps into a kitchen where Guy sets me down on a cluttered counter.

Okay. So the is s more like what I was expecting.

There is stuff everywhere: a mountain of clothes, an avalanche of letters, a teetering book stack and a whole lot of junk—opened tins and jars, an unwrapped block of butter, a half-eaten apple, an unwashed mug, a three-stringed guitar with more strings draped like spaghetti over the back of a stool...I take a breath. Okay, so it's not quite so charming in here as it was on the outside, and perhaps I'm a bit of a tidiness freak, but I like to know where everything is. That's not a crime. I hope that this chaos is not some sort of reflection of the type of person he really is...But still this is...cool. I'm cool with his bohemian. I'm open to being...more...open.

Guy swivels me around so my foot is over the kitchen sink. He removes the guitar he's carrying and leans it up against the wall while

I try not to be completely derailed by the fact that my filthy foot is now in his kitchen sink.

"What now?" I ask, leaning back and trying not to think about ecoli and bacteria and attempt to focus on looking suitably sex-kittenish. Perhaps I should try purring.

"Now I take care of you," he says — Were more romantic words ever uttered? — wetting a dishcloth, wringing it out, and gently prodding my foot.

I yelp. And sit up. My eyes follow his every move as he fills the sink with water, peers at my grubby feet and pulls a face to confirm just how unsexy they are.

Nervous laughter bubbles out of me. *Now then, Alice. Be casual. Be confident. Be sexy.* I attempt to recapture my former sexy-diva vibe.

Staring into my eyes, Guy slowly and deliberately pushes the hem of my dress up my thighs. "Wouldn't want it getting wet," he murmurs.

My breath catches and my thighs clench. I don't give a damn about getting it wet. Feeling brave, I lean in to kiss him, but mouth twitching, he leans back out of reach.

"Feet first." Guy lowers my injured foot into the warm water, which swirls grey and pink. He carefully wipes away grime and I writhe like a cut snake.

'What is this? Do you have a foot fetish?" I tease.

"Not yet..." His lips curve upwards into a wicked grin. "The cut doesn't look too serious, but you're...very...dirty..."

All sorts of images flash through my head. Guy's mouth tenderly kissing my instep, my ankle, then slowly trailing up the inside of my leg. Guy peeling off my clothes and taking me right here on the kitchen counter—although I'm not quite sure how the logistics of that would work. Would I need to turn sideways? Or would I—

"Ouch!"

Still holding onto my foot, Guy frowns.

"It's nowt. I'm all good." Well, maybe not quite so *good* anymore. Maybe tonight I'll be a tad *bad*. My body is an erotic cocktail of pleasure and pain. *Sex kitten, sex kitten, sex kitten! I remind myself.* "You really don't need to worry about it. I'll be fine." Although I sound like I've inhaled the contents of a helium balloon.

Guy studies my foot his dark hair veiling his liquid eyes. I couldn't care less about my damn foot. Right now, I would happily have it amputated. I just want to get back to the kissing part. I want to thread my fingers through his silken hair and bring his soft lips crashing down on mine. I want to give myself to him.

"Don't move." He strides from the room.

What?

Where's he gone now? I lean back and brace myself on my hands, trying out a series of poses. It's not easy, perched up here. I suck in my stomach and lean back a bit further…until my arms begin to shake. Bloody hell. I'm not sure I'm cut out to be a sex kitten.

I barely have a chance to rearrange my hair and gather my wits before Guy comes striding back in, towel slung over one shoulder, brandishing a red plastic first-aid kit. "Found it!" He lifts my foot from the water and gently dries it.

"You're going to ruin your towel," I say. Good one, Alice. Oh, so sexy.

"Hmmm." Guy inspects the sole of my foot, dries it and then applies a plaster. Eyes fixed on my face, he lifts my foot and kisses my instep. "Better?"

"Arggh!" I'm very ticklish. I attempt to jerk my leg away, but he holds it fast in his grip.

Despite being lean, he's strong. His forearms are corded with muscle. "Not so fast. Give me your other foot."

"You've got to be kidding. My other foot is fine!"

"It needs washing."

"I thought you said you approved of dirty."

"That rather depends on what we're referring to." Smiling softly, he runs clean water into the sink.

Enough already. "You're a sadist!"

His dimples appear. He eases my good foot into the sink, then gently begins to massage it with the warm soapy water.

"Oh...oh! Oh! That's...ahh...Mee-ooowh!" There's no stopping the mewling, but that's about as far as my sex-kitten impression goes.

His wicked smile broadens, and I crumple. With Guy between my legs, my red silk evening dress rucked up around my hips, my damaged foot dangling behind him and my other foot in his very capable hands, I'm ready for anything...

·

Want to find out what happens next? The sequel, 'Alice and the Impossible Game' is coming very soon (1st February 2024). Don't forget to grab your preorder bargain:

My Book

AFTERWORD

Dear reader,

I really hope you enjoyed Alice in Wanderlust. If you did please tell folks and if you would like to make my day (and year!), please feel free to leave a short review! It doesn't need to be long, but your feedback is invaluable to me as an author, for other readers trying to find these feel-good stories, and it helps to spread the word!

To be the first to learn about my upcoming releases sign up to my newsletter or please follow me on Bookbub (https://www.bookbub.com/authors/anna-foxkirk).

Other novellas in the Passport to Love series:
Be My Valerie
The Worst Noelle
Holly Ever After

You can also find out more about me from my Anna Foxkirk website.

My preferred social media is Instagram, so if you're an Insta fan, come and hang out with me at Anna Foxkirk on Instagram. I've also just started an account on TikTok and my handle there is @annafoxkirk

Before you go, let me wish you a happy and healthy new year wherever you may find yourself! May all your happy dreams and adventure come true.

Best wishes,

Anna

ABOUT THE AUTHOR

Voted Favorite Debut Romance Author of 2020 by the Australian Romance Readers Association, Anna Foxkirk writes contemporary romance and historical fiction full of love, laughter and happy ever after...

After gaining an MA in Modern History from St Andrew's University, Scotland and completing training at the Royal Military Academy Sandhurst, Anna served as an officer in the British military for seven years (including four operational military tours in war-torn Bosnia (one with Special Forces) and living in Edinburgh Castle). Nowadays, when she's not writing or reading, she enjoys a quiet(ish!) life working as an English and humanities teacher.

Her love of adventure, romance and humor blaze a trail through her stories.

Anna Foxkirk is an award-winning author. Her first novella, *Alice in Wanderlust*, was published in November 2020 as *Double Trouble* in the *Love and Fireworks* anthology, and in the same year she was voted Favorite Debut Romance Author of 2020 by the Australian Romance Readers Association.

If you like what you read, please leave her a short review or email her (annafoxkirk@gmail.com) to let her know

If you'd like to find out more, why not check out her website:
https://www.annafoxkirk.com
And finally, you'll also often find her on Instagram:
https://www.instagram.com/annafoxkirk/

ALSO BY ANNA FOXKIRK

Find some love, laughter and happy ever after in these other books by Anna Foxkirk:

Be My Valerie

The Worst Noelle

Holly Ever After

Coming on 1st February 2024, the sequel to *Alice in Wanderlust* and available for preorder now!

Alice and the Impossible Game

Printed in Great Britain
by Amazon